The Ridiculous and Wonderful Rainbow Hat

by Aaron Starmer
illustrated by Courtney La Forest

To Jacob, Will, Matteo,
and Mauro—AS

For my brother Henry and
my sister Emma—who are
always down to create some
epic pranks :)—CLF

PENGUIN WORKSHOP
An Imprint of Penguin Random House LLC, New York

Photo credits: pages 139–46 (box, calculator, piggy bank, plane, tickets) justinroque/iStock/ Getty Images Plus, (money) Yuriy Altukhov/iStock/Getty Images Plus

Text copyright © 2020 by Aaron Starmer. Illustrations copyright © 2020 by Penguin Random House LLC. All rights reserved. Published by Penguin Workshop, an imprint of Penguin Random House LLC, New York. PENGUIN and PENGUIN WORKSHOP are trademarks of Penguin Books Ltd, and the W colophon is a registered trademark of Penguin Random House LLC. Manufactured in China.

Visit us online at www.penguinrandomhouse.com.

Library of Congress Cataloging-in-Publication Data is available upon request.

ISBN 9780593222881 (pbk)   10 9 8 7 6 5 4 3 2 1
ISBN 9780593222294 (hc)   10 9 8 7 6 5 4 3 2 1

Chapter One

PREDICTABILITY

"You're predictable."

The words burned in Riley Zimmerman's mind.

Her best friend, Carson Cooper, had said those words to her a week before, and she had been thinking about them constantly. Because they were wrong.

Riley Zimmerman was not predictable. She was sure of it. Because predictable people aren't unique.

And if Riley Zimmerman was one thing, she was unique. Not *very* unique, or *a little* unique, because that's not possible. The word *unique* doesn't play well with adverbs. *Unique* means one of a kind, and a person can't be *very* one of a kind or *a little* one of a kind. They can be unique. Full stop. And that's exactly what Riley was. There was no one else like her.

Which, for Hopewell Elementary, was a good thing. That school wouldn't have lasted a week with more than one Riley roaming its halls. After all, it barely lasted a day when—

Well, we're getting to that.

First, let's start with Ping-Pong balls. Riley had ten thousand of them. And she was going to use them to prove Carson wrong.

She lived within walking distance of the school and arrived early one autumn morning. Before the first bell rang, Riley hurried back and forth from her house to the school, dragging ten bumpy trash bags filled with a thousand Ping-Pong balls each. She set the bumpy trash bags against the back wall of the school, where there used to be a dumpster, and she waited for the janitor, Reggie Blue, to unlock the rear exit.

This was part of Reggie's morning routine, something Riley knew because she had recently become a member of the Junior Janitor Club. She now had access to secret knowledge.

When she heard the click of the lock, she counted to one hundred so she could be confident the coast was clear. She took a deep breath. Then she smuggled the bags down to the basement of Hopewell Elementary and into the Dungeon.

Chapter Two
BEST FRIENDS

Yes, Hopewell Elementary had a Dungeon. It's not what you think. Or maybe it is what you think. If you've heard of Hopewell Elementary, then you've heard of the Dungeon. It was a bathroom that was super old and super gross and full of spiderwebs and creaky sounds, and no one actually used it for standard bathroom purposes. It was mostly a place for fourth-graders to find privacy, or to talk about Locker 37.

If you've heard of Hopewell Elementary, then you've definitely heard of Locker 37. It was a magical locker that provided solutions to fourth-graders' problems. It's not an exaggeration to say that Locker 37 was the universe's most wondrous creation.

We're getting to Locker 37, too.

For now, let's focus on the Dungeon: an awful bathroom, but an excellent hiding place. Also, the ideal location to feed Ping-Pong balls into the school's heating ducts.

That's exactly what Riley was doing on that chilly morning before homeroom. She had opened a vent on a wall in the corner and was pouring the bags of Ping-Pong balls in.

This was not something Riley did every day, of course. She was a master of mischief, but she had never attempted anything so ambitious. Or risky. If she were caught, it would mean a swift and significant punishment.

But here's the thing: Riley could always think or talk her way out of a jam. Even she would admit she was predictable in one way. She never got caught.

Until . . .

"What the heck are you doing?" a voice said.

Riley swung around and spilled a bag of Ping-Pong balls. They bounced around the Dungeon like popcorn in a hot pan.

"Oh, it's only you," she said when she

saw it was Carson Cooper. "Do you have a stain on your shirt you need to wash out?"

This was not an unreasonable question. Carson was basically a stain magnet. But not today.

"You sent me a message last night and asked me to meet you here," he said.

"Oh yeah," Riley said. "So here's the deal. Last week, you said I was predictable. And I simply won't accept that."

"You're missing the point," Carson responded with a sigh. "You wanted me to help you with another prank when I had homework to do. You seem to always forget that I can't drop everything to do exactly what you want me to do. So I said you were predictable. It's—"

"Unpredictable," Riley said with a finger up. "I'm unpredictable. I'm unique, and unique people can't be predictable. Because who else would ever do what I'm doing?"

"What are you doing?"

"I'm filling the heating ducts with ten thousand Ping-Pong balls. That way, when the heat turns on, all the balls will shoot out into the hallways and classrooms and it will be the greatest prank Hopewell Elementary has ever seen. Now, that's unpredictable."

"That's . . . irresponsible."

"Only if I don't do it right," Riley said. "So now that I've let you in on my greatest, most brilliant prank, all I need you to do is remove the screws on a bunch of the school's heating vents."

Carson stood there for a moment, staring at Riley with a look of either wonder or disgust—it was hard to tell which. Then he turned around and left the Dungeon.

"Does that mean you won't help me?" Riley called out.

But she already knew the answer.

She'd have to find someone else.

Chapter Three

ACCOMPLICES?

"Listen," Riley whispered to Bryce Dodd in homeroom. "All I need you to do is loosen a few screws."

Bryce nodded and said, "You always tell me that I have a few screws loose, don't you?"

Riley handed him a screwdriver. "When I say that about you, it's a compliment. Means you're . . .

unpredictable. Like me."

Bryce handed the screwdriver back. "I predict that this will get me in trouble, so I have to say sorry, but I can't do it. Why don't you ask Keisha?"

Riley laughed out loud, which caught the attention of her homeroom teacher, Mrs. Shen.

"I'd ask you to share your joke with the class, but I might end up regretting it," Mrs. Shen said.

"I'm sorry," Riley said. "It was Bryce. He said the most absurd thing in the universe. That's all."

Bryce shrugged innocently.

Meanwhile, Keisha James, who was sprinkling fish food into the bowl of the class goldfish, said, "I don't think it's possible to say the most absurd thing in the universe. You'd need a planet of supercomputers to calculate even a fraction of that absurdity."

Riley considered this and then replied, "What if I said that you, Keisha James, would be sent to Vice Principal Meehan's office today for breaking the rules?"

Keisha didn't have to even consider this. She was, after all, the fourth grade's biggest perfectionist. She simply said, "Okay, that is the most absurd thing in the universe. Carry on."

Riley turned back to Bryce and said, "And there you have it."

Mrs. Shen walked to the front of the room and turned on the whiteboard. "I don't have a clue what any of you are talking about . . . but I do have a clue to share," she said as she pointed to a picture on the whiteboard of three colorful circles. "There will be no science class today."

Cheers erupted from the class.

"But that doesn't mean we won't be learning something," she went on. "We are having an assembly. Can you guess what it's about?"

There were more cheers, but there were also a few worried whispers. Assemblies were sometimes fun, but sometimes they were a bit weird. Like the time a professional pig caller did a demonstration, and proceeded to scream "Soooey!" into a microphone for a good ten minutes. Or—

"It's not another author coming to tell us about some boring book he wrote, is it?" Hunter Barnes said.

Hunter was not a fan of authors, or reading, or education in general, unless that education involved learning ways to insult and annoy his classmates. He was the school's most ruthless bully.

"And why do these circles make you think of an author?" Mrs. Shen asked.

"I don't know," Hunter said. "Circles are boring and authors are boring."

Mrs. Shen glared at Hunter for a moment and then turned to the class. "Any other guesses?"

"I'm not getting an award, am I?" Keisha asked. "Do the circles represent three first-place medals?"

"Interesting theory . . . ," Mrs. Shen said. "But no."

That's when Sarah Abramson jumped to her feet. She had an eraser, her watch, and a hat in her hands. She began to juggle them because, well, Sarah Abramson was an amazing juggler and loved juggling. She had also discovered the right answer.

"Bingo!" Mrs. Shen said. "We have a troupe of jugglers that will entertain us as a reward for everyone's hard work."

Now the cheers were deafening, because the kids assumed there was nothing educational about juggling.

But Riley didn't cheer. Instead, she whispered to herself, "Holy fusilli. This changes things."

It meant her prank would now be infinitely better. Completely, entirely, utterly unpredictable. Something Carson couldn't possibly ignore. The problem was, it also meant her prank would now be infinitely harder, especially since no one was willing to be her accomplice.

There was only one place to turn.

Locker 37.

Chapter Four

LOCKER 37

O kay, back to Locker 37.

Locker 37 was awesome. Amazing. Incredible. And perhaps it had a few screws loose, too, because it was also unpredictable.

Actually, there was at least one thing about it you could predict. If you were a fourth-grader at Hopewell Elementary and you had a problem, you could open

Locker 37 and it would provide a solution.

Locker 37 had been performing this essential service for the school's fourth-graders for more than fifty years, and only fourth-graders knew about it. No one told the younger kids, and everyone older forgot about Locker 37 as soon as they moved on to fifth grade. That was all part of the locker's magic. But the most important part of its magic was that it gave out magical objects.

Sometimes those objects provided obvious solutions to problems.

Like once, when a kid scraped his knee on the playground, Locker 37 gave him a tube of cream that would heal any wound, no matter how big or oozy.

There was a Hula-Hoop waiting in

Locker 37 for another kid. It made the kid fly when she spun it around her body, which helped her retrieve her field trip permission slip that had blown up into a tree.

And Locker 37 even gave one kid a little wallet with a check inside that paid off all overdue balances on his friends' lunch accounts.

But remember, Locker 37 was unpredictable. The solutions it provided weren't always obvious ones. The previous year's fourth-graders explained this in a note about Locker 37 that they left for Carson, Riley, and their friends.

It won't always be the solution you want, or expect, but it is guaranteed to work.

Riley's problem wasn't as gross, or as simple, or as noble as other problems kids had had in the past. She wanted to show her best friend, and the world, that she was unpredictable by pulling off the greatest prank in the history of Hopewell Elementary. But she didn't have anyone who was willing to help her.

So, what object did Riley find when she opened Locker 37?

What object was supposed to provide the solution to that problem?

A hat, of course.

Chapter Five

A HAT BOTH RIDICULOUS AND WONDERFUL

The hat was a ridiculous hat. It was also wonderful. But you already knew that because you read the book's title. And the chapter title. So let's get more specific.

It was a rainbow-colored hat. It had a brim and pom-poms and a bunch of feathers and ribbons. It had stripes and polka dots. It was a combination of mesh and wool and denim. It was an absolute mess of a hat, the type of thing anyone would be embarrassed to wear. Except maybe Riley.

"Well, hello, greatest hat ever!" Riley said as she opened Locker 37 and saw it sitting inside the locker's orange glow.

The words "Wear Me" were stitched on the brim, but she hardly needed the encouragement. She immediately put it on her head, and when she did, she heard a voice behind her.

"Well, hello, greatest person ever," the voice said.

Riley swung around and saw . . . Riley.

She was looking at herself. Not a mirror image, because the Riley she was looking at wasn't mirroring her movements. The original Riley was standing perfectly still and staring at this new Riley, who was jumping up and down.

"So cool!" the new Riley cheered. "There are two of me!"

This was true. The new Riley was an exact replica of the original Riley, except for one difference: the ridiculous and wonderful hat. The new Riley wore the same style hat, but hers wasn't rainbow colored. It was entirely green.

The original Riley broke out of her daze and tore off the rainbow hat.

The new Riley froze in place.

Her eyes were half blinking; her mouth was half-open. It was like she was a robot and someone had pressed

the pause button on her.

"Holy linguine, I made a clone," Riley said to herself. And to her frozen self.

Then she put the hat back on. And the Riley clone started moving again. But that wasn't all.

"Hey there, you two," said a voice from behind them.

The original Riley swung around, and the Riley with the green hat swung around, and they both found another Riley standing in the hallway. This newest Riley was exactly the same as the others, only she was wearing a blue hat.

If you're keeping track, that's three Rileys in total: the original (rainbow hat) and two clones (green hat and blue hat).

"Holy linguine with clam sauce, I'm

cloning up a storm," Riley said. "I better pace myself."

The eyebrows of both clones went up, then they each put a hand in front of their mouths to hide their devious smiles.

"First things first," the original Riley said as she let a smile slip out, too. "To avoid confusion, I'm going to call you Green Me and Blue Me. Everyone okay with that?"

The clones looked at each other and shrugged. Green Riley said, "Call us anything you want."

Blue Riley followed that up by saying, "As long as you've got some mischief for us to do."

"Oh, that . . . can be arranged," Original Riley told them.

Chapter Six

MORE, MORE, MORE

Riley took the rainbow hat off and put it back on two more times, which taught her the rules:

1. Every time she took the hat off, her clones would freeze in place.
2. When she put it back on, the clones would start moving again, and . . .
3. . . . a new clone would appear.

So now she had four clones with four different-colored hats. There was Green Riley, Blue Riley, Orange Riley, and Red Riley. Fortunately, Locker 37 was wise enough not to give cloning powers to clones. Their hats couldn't freeze or create anything. They could take them off and put them on all they wanted. They preferred to keep them on, though. They thought they were fashionable. And it helped them tell one another apart.

"Okay," Riley told her clones. "There's work to do, but there's also a problem. It's time for gym class. I have to go alone, or that might be . . . suspicious."

"Cool," Blue Riley said. "I'll just sneak into the teachers' lounge and switch the sugar next to the coffee with salt."

"Oooh, I'm gonna go get that drone that Dad has in the shed, put a witch costume and a broom on it, and chase kids through the halls," Red Riley said.

"I've got a better idea," Original Riley told them. "Follow me to the Dungeon."

The Riley clones liked the sound of that, and they rubbed their hands together in anticipation.

Getting down there without being seen was another matter entirely. First period was about to start and kids were leaving homeroom. The hall next to Locker 37 was empty for now, but to get to the Dungeon, they had to travel down one of the school's busiest halls.

Luckily, the art room was nearby. And Riley had a plan.

Chapter Seven

SAINT RILEY'S DAY

"Parade coming through!" Riley shouted as she and her clones exited the art room.

The four clones still wore their ridiculous hats, but now they also wore colorful paintings over their faces.

On the first day of school, Riley had painted a series of self-portraits in art class. By attaching rubber bands to them, the Rileys had turned them into masks. The "self-portrait" masks actually looked more like animals than they did like Riley. But they hid the clones' faces as they marched down the hall, slapping their thighs in rhythm and pretending this was a parade.

"And what exactly is this parade for, Miss Zimmerman?" Vice Principal Meehan asked Riley, who was the only one not wearing a mask.

"Saint Riley's Day, of course," Riley told him.

By the time Meehan figured out that there was no such thing as Saint Riley's Day, they were already around the corner.

They sang a song as they marched.

Saint Riley's Day, Saint Riley's Day,
The best day of the year.
A day to proudly shout hooray,
Saint Riley's Day is here!
Saint Riley's Day, Saint Riley's Day,
It's really very cool.
It should be a holiday,
They ought to cancel school!

Sometimes the best way not to be noticed is to draw attention to yourself. Or something like that. At least that was the logic behind the Rileys' plan.

They almost got away with it, too. That is, until they were walking down the stairs toward the Dungeon, and Hunter Barnes passed them on the way.

His eyes were red and his cheeks were damp, as if he'd been crying. The moment he saw the group of Rileys, he sniffled and sneered and asked, "What's with the ugly mugs?"

Then he ripped the mask from Blue Riley's face.

The parade stopped dead in its tracks. This was not good.

The original Riley tried to distract

Hunter by doing the one thing bullies usually can't handle: bullying back.

"What's with *your* mug?" she said in a teasing tone. "I caught you crying, didn't I, Hunter?"

She immediately felt guilty. It was a very mean thing to say. Entirely uncalled-for. And besides, it didn't work. Because it didn't distract Hunter at all.

"There are two of you," he said with a gasp.

"Five of me, actually," the other clones said. Since they were already caught, they figured there was no harm in revealing themselves.

As they removed their masks, Hunter's eyes darted from face to identical face, and he said, "I'm supposed to faint right now, aren't I?"

He didn't faint. Because he was a fourth-grader, and fourth-graders at Hopewell Elementary were accustomed to seeing strange things like this.

Instead of fainting, Hunter stood there gawking at the ridiculous and wonderful hats they wore. That is, until the original Riley grabbed his sleeve.

"Come on," she said. "We can't be spotted. We've got to get you and each and every one of me to the Dungeon."

Chapter Eight

WHAT WE TALK ABOUT WHEN WE TALK ABOUT CLONING

Clones are cool. Let's admit that first.

Two of you? Three of you? One hundred of you? That'd make life easier and the world a better place, right?

Ummm . . . maybe.

You see, there's something else we have to admit.

Clones are scary. Does the world

really need more than one of you? Don't take this the wrong way — you're simply amazing — but perhaps there can be too much of a good thing.

Because clones aren't always what they seem. They seem like perfect copies, but are they actually?

Yes. And no.

Not the most helpful answer, obviously, so maybe it's time to get a little more in depth on what a clone actually is.

Clones of animals (and remember, humans *are* animals) share the exact same DNA. DNA is short for deoxyribonucleic acid, as you probably guessed. If you didn't guess that, don't worry. All you need to know is that every animal has microscopic strands of DNA inside their bodies, and those strands are the instructions that tell their bodies how to grow.

This means that a clone of an animal will start with the exact same instructions as the original animal. Those instructions will determine things like hair color, eye color, maybe even whether the animal enjoys eating fish sticks or not. But just because a clone has the exact same DNA as the original animal, it doesn't mean the two will do the exact same things.

For example, let's say Riley went for a walk in the woods with one of her clones. And let's say the two of them came upon a bear.

If Riley told her clone, "Let's go tickle that bear!" the clone might have second thoughts, right?

I know I have identical DNA to Riley, the clone might think. *But bear tickling seems a wee bit iffy. Don't get me wrong. I'd love to hear a bear giggle. Who wouldn't? But what about the teeth? And the claws? And the overall beariness of the bear? Frankly, that worries me. And who's to say this bear is even ticklish? Is this a risk worth taking? Maybe I'll just let my DNA buddy tickle the bear and see what happens first.*

A wise clone, indeed. Because what would happen?

Well, odds are that Riley would grin and wiggle her fingers and slowly approach the puzzled bear. When she started saying, "Welcome to Tickle Town, Mr. Bear," her clone would probably turn and start walking very swiftly in the other direction.

Any growling, screaming, and chewing sounds that Riley's clone might hear as she hurried away would confirm that even if two people share the same DNA, it doesn't mean they will both be eaten by a humorless bear.

So instead of thinking of clones as exact copies, think of clones as different versions of the same song.

Most songs have defined music and lyrics. In other words, this is what you play and this is what you sing. The music and lyrics are essentially the DNA of the song. The instructions!

But once that song gets into the hands of different musicians, there are different interpretations of the instructions. It's still the same song, but each version has a unique sound.

Of course, it must be pointed out that Riley's clones were a bit different from traditional clones. They popped into existence as fully grown fourth-graders. They shared Riley's DNA but also her memories up until the moment she opened Locker 37.

But they were still like songs. The performances might have been exactly the same up through the first verse and chorus, but now that they were on their own, they were free to find their own sound. Which leads to an inevitable question.

Was that a good thing?

Yes. And no.

Chapter Nine

CUTTIN' ONIONS

"So, as you can see, Locker 37 gave me a magic hat that makes clones," Riley told Hunter Barnes in the Dungeon.

"Uh . . . yeah," Hunter said as he stared at the four other Rileys in their ridiculous and wonderful red, blue, orange, and green hats.

"And, as *I* can see, you've been crying," Riley said.

"No, I haven't," Hunter replied.

"I see it, too," Red Riley said.

"And crying is fine," Orange Riley said.

"It's good, actually," Blue Riley said.

"Everyone should cry every once in a while," Green Riley said.

"Hey, let me speak for myself," Original Riley told the others.

They all shrugged and quieted down.

"Actually, I agree with . . . them . . . or me . . . or whatever," Riley said. "It's okay to cry. It's good. And I'm not going to tell anyone that you were—"

"I wasn't crying!" Hunter shouted. "I was cuttin' onions!"

They all stood in silence for a few moments, because this was certainly not an excuse they expected.

"Really?" Riley finally asked.

"Really," Hunter said.

"And why were you cutting onions?" Riley asked.

"None of your business," Hunter said.

Of course, Riley didn't believe that he was cutting onions, because what fourth-grader spends his morning cutting onions? But she wasn't going to call him a liar, because she needed him to stay quiet. Hunter was a notorious blabbermouth.

"Listen," she said. "I'm guessing you have a problem. I do, too. And I could use your help. Let's help each other."

The other Rileys grimaced at this proposal. They knew Hunter's reputation for trustworthiness. Which was he had none. No one trusted him.

"Do I get to use the hat?" Hunter asked, and he grabbed at it, wrapping his fingers around a rainbow-colored ribbon.

"No way!" Riley shouted as she put both hands on top of the hat to keep it in place. As she yanked it away from Hunter, she thought she heard the seams ripping—*oh no!*—but she managed to keep the hat firmly planted on her head and out of his grasp.

Hunter sneered, stuffed his hands in his pockets, and asked, "Then do I get to use one of your clones?"

"No!" all the other Rileys said at once.

"Jeez," Hunter said. "Then this doesn't sound like a good deal for me."

"It will be," Riley said, and she reached into her pocket and pulled out a single Ping-Pong ball she'd been holding on to as a souvenir. "Do you know what this is?"

"Sure," Hunter said. "I'm not stupid. That's a sea turtle egg."

Blue and Red Riley lifted their hands in front of their faces to stifle their laughter.

But the original Riley played it cool, bouncing the Ping-Pong ball on the grimy floor of the Dungeon and then catching it. "Or it might be a Ping-Pong ball."

Blood rushed to Hunter's face as he mumbled, "Right. That's my nickname for

Ping-Pong balls: sea turtle eggs."

"Whatever you say," Riley told him.
"Now, try to imagine ten thousand of
these . . . sea turtle eggs . . . and they're
shooting out from the heating vent
above the gym and raining down on our
classmates and teachers."

"As well as professional jugglers,"
Orange Riley added.

"As well as professional jugglers,"
Riley echoed. "The . . . sea turtle eggs . . .
are bouncing and causing all sorts of
mayhem. Is that something you'd like to
see?"

Hunter grinned. And nodded.

"Good," Riley said. "So this is what you
have to do."

Chapter Ten

FORESHADOWING

Here's the thing about authors.

They're not always nice. They're downright cruel sometimes.

They withhold information for the sake of telling a "better" story.

That's what's going on here. You won't be told what Riley asked Hunter to do. At least not until the end of the book. The author thinks that's for your own good, and that you'll enjoy the story more if you wait to hear the best parts.

Isn't that simply terrible?

Don't throw the book across the room just yet, though. Because there is something you can do about it. It will, however, require a bit of investigative work.

You see, there are clues sprinkled throughout the book. These clues can help you figure out what Riley asked Hunter to do and what Hunter actually did.

Hiding clues about what will be revealed later in a story is known as *foreshadowing*. It is defined as "an indication of what is to come," but mostly it's a dirty trick that authors use to taunt readers.

Again: simply terrible.

But you're smarter than any author, aren't you? Or you're at least smarter than this particular author. You can figure out his tricky and terrible foreshadowing and predict what will happen.

All you have to do is focus on all the details in this book. Ponder the images. Pay particular attention to specific words. They may be hinting at something that's going to occur later.

Not to drone on and on about this, but there are more than one hundred

pages left that will shed a light on what Hunter did. Don't fly by every other word without considering how they might contribute to this beautiful symphony of ideas. Don't rip through the pages simply to reach the end. Just hold on to your hat, focus your eyes, and beat this author at his own game.

Got all that? Good.

Moving on.

Chapter Eleven
INFESTATION

After Hunter left the Dungeon to do what you'll unfortunately have to hear about later, Riley gave her clones their assignments. Then they all split off in separate directions.

Red Riley's job was to hide out in the utility room and monitor the furnace to make sure the heat didn't come on until the exact right moment.

Green Riley went to the playground, where she was expected to hide in a tree and listen in on her classmates to collect any gossip that might help their mission.

Blue Riley was supposed to station herself in a stall in the Dungeon, to make sure the Ping-Pong balls weren't discovered.

Orange Riley, designated as a free agent, was told to wait inside Riley's locker for more instructions.

And Original Riley hurried to first period, which was gym.

Keisha James was on a bench in the gym locker room, lacing her shoes, when Riley burst in. Keisha looked up and said, "Nice hat, buddy. But you're late."

"By your calculations, maybe," Riley replied.

"By the clock's calculations, actually," Keisha said, pointing to the clock above the door leading to the gym. "You have exactly thirty seconds before you have to be out on the floor, or Mr. Trundle will mark you absent. You can't get ready in thirty seconds."

"Not true," Riley said as she grabbed her pair of neon-green gym shorts from her pocket and then pulled them on over her baggy jeans. "*You* can't get ready in thirty seconds."

Then she sprinted into the gym.

"Well, good morning, Riley," Mr. Trundle said as she emerged from the locker room. "Interesting attire you've chosen for today.

Especially the . . . headgear."

"Can I help it that I'm an exceedingly interesting person?" she replied, though she resisted the temptation to tip her hat, because she didn't need to be creating another clone at the moment.

Mr. Trundle rolled his eyes. "Lose the hat."

"I'd love to," Riley said. "But I have to wear it or something terrible might happen."

"Such as?"

Riley thought over her choice of words, then finally settled on a single one: "Infestation."

Mr. Trundle assumed she was talking about some creepy-crawly things in her hair. Mr. Trundle most definitely did not like creepy-crawly things. So he put his hands up and took a step back. "Say no more. You can wear what you're wearing today, but maybe it's time for a haircut."

"Maybe," Riley said, even though she loved her wild mane and would never consider chopping it off.

"And next class, please stick to only shorts," Mr. Trundle added. "No jeans underneath."

"Roger that," Riley replied, and she pointed at him with both index fingers.

But here's the thing: She wasn't simply wearing her jeans to save time. Little did Mr. Trundle know that Riley had a trick up her sleeve.

Or, to be more precise, a fishing rod and reel up her baggy pants leg.

Chapter Twelve

PARACHUTE DAY

Riley didn't always keep a fishing rod and reel duct-taped to her leg, but today was the sort of day when she thought she might need one. And, boy, was she right.

You see, for Riley's prank to succeed, she needed to open the heating vent in the gym.

In the past, there was a climbing rope that led right up to the ceiling, giving climbers easy access to the vent. But the rope was no longer there, so reaching the vent would now be significantly more difficult.

Of course, Riley had only herself to blame for this hiccup in the plan.

On the first day of school, she had shinnied up the climbing rope and erased the heating vent (using a magic eraser from Locker 37, obviously). It had caused a legendary rain of Madagascar hissing cockroaches on a class of unsuspecting second-graders, as such things often do.

Riley was never punished, because she replaced the vent before anyone could prove she had done anything wrong. But to make sure there were no more cockroach rains, Mr. Trundle took the climbing rope down. That meant the heating vent was now at least thirty feet from the floor, the walls, or anything that could be climbed to touch it.

Fortunately, Riley knew that she didn't actually have to touch the vent to open it. She only had to make it wiggle. That's because there was a loose latch holding it shut. If the vent wiggled enough, the loose latch would turn and—*voilà!*—the vent would fall open.

This was where the fishing rod and reel came into the equation.

Thirty feet may have been an impossible distance to reach or jump, but it was a relatively short distance to cast a fishing line.

Riley knew if she could hook the vent with the fishing line, she could wiggle the vent.

If she could wiggle the vent, she could open the vent.

And if she could open the vent, then the Ping-Pong balls would have their escape route, directly above the students, teachers, and jugglers.

The prank would be a ping-ponging success!

Of course, there was one more hiccup in the plan. Riley needed some time alone to cast the line and hook the vent. And Mr. Trundle never, ever left the gym. (Unless it was raining Madagascar hissing cockroaches.)

She needed a miracle. She needed—

"Today is parachute day!" Mr. Trundle announced.

The announcement was met with great excitement from the class, with shouts of "Yeah, baby!" and "My most glorious dreams have come true!" echoing throughout the gym.

It was also met with a sigh of relief from Riley. Parachute day was *exactly* what she needed.

But what was parachute day?

Well, it was the one day every few months when Mr. Trundle brought out the giant rainbow-colored parachute. He was particularly good at coming up with new parachute games for the class to play. He'd use rubber balls (Popcorn Party!), jump ropes (Snakenado!), and other things found in the gym (Bowling Pin Hula-Hoop Pommel Horse Parachute Extravaganza!).

Most importantly, at least for Riley, Mr. Trundle would always do the same thing at the end of each parachute day.

He'd shout, "CIRCUS TENT!" and everyone in class, including Mr. Trundle, would create a big tent out of the parachute. Then they'd scurry under it, count down from one hundred, and not come out until they reached zero (or until the parachute completely deflated).

That moment, when everyone was beneath the fabric, would be Riley's best chance to use her fishing rod and reel. And it would last, at most, one hundred seconds.

Chapter Thirteen
FISHING

"One, two, three . . . CIRCUS TENT!" Mr. Trundle shouted as the rainbow-colored parachute puffed up and the children scrambled underneath it.

Riley ducked her shoulder and faked like she was going to scramble underneath, but she remained on the outside, where she sprang into action. She pulled up her pants leg and tore the duct tape off her skin. She put one hand over her mouth to muffle any cries of pain. But she didn't have to. The kids counting under the parachute were so loud that she could have screamed at the top of her lungs and no one would have noticed.

"Ninety-nine! Ninety-eight! Ninety-seven . . ."

The fishing rod and reel were in three pieces. She had to assemble them. Luckily, she had practiced at home and could do it in fifteen seconds.

"Eighty-two! Eighty-one! Eighty . . ."

Next, she had to attach the lure to the end of the fishing line. Because while she was willing to take some risks, she wasn't willing to keep the lure attached to the line and hidden down her pants. The thing had three barbed hooks on it!

Instead, she had the lure stored in a small jewelry box in her pocket. Pulling it out and attaching it to the line took another ten seconds.

"Seventy! Sixty-nine! Sixty-eight . . ."

Now all that was left was to position herself, take a deep breath, focus on her target, use the fishing rod to cast the lure, miss all the rafters and banners and pipes in the way, and hook the vent that was thirty feet above her head, and she had about—*"Fifty-nine! Fifty-eight! Fifty-seven . . ."*—seconds left to do it!

"Here goes," she whispered to herself, and she lowered the fishing rod and flung it forward. The lure went sailing through the air and missed the vent by about

eight feet, hitting the ceiling and falling to the floor.

Riley reeled the lure in and got ready to try again.

"Forty-six! Forty-five! Forty-four . . ."

That morning, when she was taping the rod and reel to her leg, she thought she'd use them to hook a few hallway heating vents that were a tiny bit out of reach. She never suspected she'd have to cast the lure thirty feet through the gym!

Riley wished she had brought her dad's drone with her instead. Her dad kept a small black one in the family's shed, next to an ancient boom box that he used to play classical music, and a chest freezer filled with frozen fish sticks. Taping a drone to her leg wasn't possible, of course, but if Riley had brought the drone, she could've flown it up to the vent and given it a shake. Easy peasy.

What she could've done didn't matter, though. All that mattered was what she could actually do, which was cast that lure. It was hard, but she wasn't giving up. She figured she had enough time for maybe three more tries.

She lowered the fishing rod, and as she was flinging it—

"My turn!" someone shouted.

The lure flew off course, clanging against a pipe in the ceiling that was at least fifteen feet from her target.

"Holy acini di pepe!" Orange Riley cried.

"What are you doing here?" Original Riley asked.

Orange Riley stood a few feet away, shrugging. "I was bored. Thought I'd come fishing."

"I can't . . . you can't . . . I mean, I can't . . . other versions of me can't be here," Riley said as she reeled the line back in.

"Thirty-three! Thirty-two! Thirty-one . . ."

"Well, I *am* here," Orange Riley said. "So, technically, I *can* be here."

"So can I," Red Riley announced as she stepped into the gym and joined Orange Riley's side.

"Go hide!" Riley told them. "There isn't much—"

"Twenty-five! Twenty-four! Twenty-three . . ."

"But I want a turn," Orange Riley said as she grabbed for the fishing rod.

Riley pulled the rod away from Orange Riley, but then it ended up right in Red Riley's hands.

"Bet I can hook that grate," Red Riley said as she yanked at the pole.

Riley yanked it back. "I'm ... you're ... everything is going to be ruined!"

"Thirteen! Twelve! Eleven ..."

The parachute was nearly deflated. The heads of her classmates were creating bumps on its surface, like bubbles on a field of rainbow lava. In ten seconds, those heads would emerge and the eyes in those heads would see Riley, her fishing rod and reel, and two of her clones.

She had to think fast.

With all her strength, Riley tore the fishing rod away from Red Riley. She drew it back and cast the lure. Only, she wasn't aiming for the grate.

"Seven! Six! Five ..."

"Get ready to run," Riley told the clones

as the lure struck the parachute and hooked the fabric.

"Three! Two! One!"

Then she yanked the rod as hard as she could, pulling the parachute off her classmates and sending it sailing over her own head.

Before her classmates realized what was happening, the parachute landed on top of Red Riley and Orange Riley, hiding them from view. Then the original Riley pointed at the parachute and the two lumps beneath it.

"It's getting away!" she screamed.

The clones ran.

Chapter Fourteen

THE RAINBOW SPECTER

"**W**ho is that?" Mr. Trundle asked Riley as her two clones, covered in the rainbow-colored parachute, barreled out of the gym and into the hallway, dragging the fishing rod with them.

"Maybe it was me," Riley said with a shrug, because sometimes telling the truth is the easiest way to throw someone off your scent. Or something like that. At least that was the logic behind Riley's plan.

Mr. Trundle's eyes narrowed. "Enough joking," he said, and he quickly counted the kids. "I know it was none of my students, because everyone is here."

"This is clearly a disaster," Carson announced as he paced around the gym. "If the parachute is stolen, there might never be another parachute day again!"

He might as well have announced that the clones had taken the world's last pint of ice cream. Parachute-day-loving fourth-graders (which was all of them) were suddenly hot on the trail of Red Riley and Orange Riley, stampeding from the gym into the hall.

"Class isn't over yet!" Mr. Trundle shouted, but no one paid attention. The bell would ring soon enough, and he wasn't about to punish the entire class for trying to stop parachute thieves.

Not that the class was thinking that far ahead. They simply wanted the parachute back.

Riley wanted the opposite, of course, though she couldn't let her classmates know that. So she joined the mob, but she ran alongside Bryce, the most . . . open-minded of her classmates.

"I didn't want to say this earlier and scare everyone," she told him as they ran. "But do you realize that we're chasing a ghost right now?"

"Like, a phantom?" Bryce asked.

"Yep."

"A spirit?"

"Uh-huh."

"A rainbow specter?"

"Indeed," Riley said. "I tried to catch it with a fishing rod. No luck. Problem is, if anyone touches it, that would be bad news."

"What would happen?" Bryce asked.

"Ever put a marshmallow in the microwave?" Riley asked.

Bryce smiled and nodded.

"It's not exactly that," Riley said. "But, you know, it's not exactly *not* that, either."

Bryce's face dropped. He got

serious. "We have to do something."

"Any ideas?"

Riley was a genius when it came to shenanigans, but even she was occasionally stumped by sticky situations like these. Bryce, on the other hand, was a wellspring of random thoughts. No one had a mind like his.

Any other fourth-grader would have said, "Tell Vice Principal Meehan!" or, more likely, "Go to Locker 37 and it'll sort things out."

What Bryce thought up was a little different.

"We're gonna need a bunch of kindergartners," he said, and he sprinted to the head of the pack. "And you better get ready to sing."

Chapter Fifteen

IF YOU'RE HAPPY AND YOU KNOW IT

The parachute-covered clones rounded the corner and headed toward the stairway to the Dungeon, with the mob hot on their heels. Carson, Bryce, and Riley were at the front of the pack.

"We've got to stop the chase," Bryce told Carson.

"No chance," Carson said. "School is stressful enough. Parachute day is the only thing that isn't. Parachute day must live on!"

"And it will live on," Riley told him. "But we need to keep our distance."

"'Tis not wise to tangle with the supernatural," Bryce added. "Especially the rainbowed variety."

Then Bryce and Riley jumped in front of Carson and spread out their arms and legs, blocking his path. Carson stopped and scowled.

"Don't make me knock you over," he said. "Violence is not in my nature."

The rest of the kids stopped, too, and they also told Bryce and Riley to move, though the words they used weren't nearly as polite as what Carson said.

Still, Bryce and Riley stood their ground.

Because they knew what was coming.

Brrrrrrrring.

The bell signaling the end of first period echoed through the school.

Moments later, a door opened and one of the kindergarten teachers, Mr. Gorman, stepped into the hallway.

"Single file, children," Mr. Gorman said as he shepherded a line of perfectly obedient five- and six-year-olds out of his room. In no time, they filled the corridor.

"Good morning, Mr. Gorman," Carson said. "Can we ask you and your class to step to the side so that we can get past? We're currently dealing with some official fourth-grade business."

"And what exactly is *official* fourth-grade—" Mr. Gorman started to say, but

Bryce interrupted him.

"If you're happy and you know it, clap your hands!" Bryce sang.

Without missing a beat, some of the kindergartners did exactly that.

Clap clap.

You see, silly songs like this are kindergartners' greatest weakness. If you sing to them, they can't resist. And Bryce sang the full song (you know how it goes, so we won't write it all here) so all the kindergartners were fully under its spell.

Clap clap.

Then he sang a new, improvised line.

"If you're happy and you know it, lie down on the ground and wiggle like snakes and giggle and block the way even if your teacher tells you not to!"

It wasn't a perfect verse, but it worked. Sure enough, the hallway was soon filled with wiggling, giggling kindergartners who wouldn't listen as Mr. Gorman begged, "Up, children! Please! Up!"

"Looks like you'll have to find another way around," Riley told Carson and the rest of the group.

"That is, unless you want to trample some kindergartners," Bryce added. "And then end up as another marshmallowed victim of the notorious rainbow specter."

Puzzled looks swept over the crowd. Then there were shrugs, whispers of "oh, well," and kids wandering back to the locker room to change before their next class. The official fourth-grade business was officially over.

Chapter Sixteen

THE PING-PONG PLAN PROBLEM

Ping-Pong balls are unpredictable. Throw one across a room and try to guess where it will end up.

Seriously, throw a Ping-Pong ball. Right now. If you need to go to your local Ping-Pong ball factory to acquire one, that's fine. We'll wait.

Okay, so you threw the Ping-Pong ball and it bounced all over the place, didn't it? Off the wall, the floor, the table . . . the cat. Then it rolled somewhere you didn't expect, right?

Now throw ten thousand Ping-Pong balls. That's right, go back to the Ping-Pong ball factory for 9,999 more. We'll wait.

Whoa, huh?

The point is this: Riley's plan to have Ping-Pong balls burst like a geyser from the vent above the gym may have been a bit ambitious. With a maze of heating ducts, how was she going to get all ten thousand of those unpredictable things to end up in the same place? Not to mention the fact that she hadn't even gotten that vent open yet.

There are a few possibilities as to how

she might've pulled it off.

For instance, she could've injected the balls with ten thousand magnets or microrobots, or used a school-bus-size vacuum to suck the—

Yeah . . . no. The logistics and budgets for such endeavors would be so ridiculous that it's not even worth finishing that sentence.

The actual solution she would come up with was so much simpler, cheaper, and less ridiculous. Because, you see, Riley was clever and resourceful, and that's why Locker 37 gave her the hat in the first place.

Locker 37 trusted kids to solve most of their problems on their own. In some situations, it probably didn't even need to give them anything. And here's a perfect example.

Once upon a time, a girl named Lucinda Honeycutt opened Locker 37 and it was . . . empty.

Which was strange. Because she was the first fourth-grader to open the locker that morning. Unsurprisingly, Lucinda walked away with a hanging head and a yearning heart. Because she still had a problem.

Lucinda's best friend, Beatrice Vonderhauf, had challenged her to a breath-holding contest at the local pool that afternoon. "Let's time each other and see who can go for the longest," Beatrice had said. "Loser pays the winner her snack for a month."

"I'm in," Lucinda had responded.

It was an understandable response, because Beatrice Vonderhauf had the best snacks in fourth grade. Potato chips. Cupcakes. Candy! To beat Beatrice in a breath-holding contest would mean a month of pure snacking joy. But when Lucinda had agreed to the contest, she had forgotten something important.

Lucinda was deathly afraid of being underwater.

Whoops. Bad move, Lucinda.

And since Locker 37 didn't help Lucinda, she had to make a choice that afternoon at the pool.

Would she admit her fear and forfeit her snacks for a month?

Or would she face her fear and try to win those chips, and cupcakes, and candy?

She sat on the edge of the pool, holding a stopwatch, as Beatrice pinched her nose and ducked under the water.

The clock ticked.

Bubbles bubbled to the surface.

And finally, Beatrice emerged, one minute and one second later.

"Beat that, Lucinda," Beatrice said with a cough.

Lucinda stared at her friend, then down at the water, then at the stopwatch, which was stopped at one minute and one second. Then she closed her eyes for a moment and remembered the emptiness she had seen in Locker 37.

If Locker 37 wasn't going to solve her problem, it meant there was only one choice. She had to solve it by herself.

"I'll try," she told Beatrice.

Lucinda was terrified—her heart was positively pounding—but she faced her fear. She pinched her nose, slipped down under the water, and held her breath.

That was when she realized something.

Locker 37 hadn't failed her. It had, indeed, given her something. It wasn't what you would normally think of as a magical object. But it was made up of atoms and molecules and things left over from the big bang.

It was . . .

Breath!

Her lungs were full of magical breath!

She didn't see the breath when she opened the locker. But she had sucked it into her lungs, and as she sat on the bottom of the pool, she realized that she could now breathe underwater.

She could not only beat Beatrice. She could destroy her!

Lucinda could stay underwater for minutes. For hours. For days! And when she emerged, she'd have a month of delicious snacks to look forward to.

But that's not why Locker 37 had given her the breath. Her problem wasn't that she needed to win some snacks. It was that she needed to conquer her fear of being underwater. And the problem was solved when Lucinda found the courage within herself to face that fear.

Locker 37 tricked her into thinking that it wasn't going to help her. But it did help her, in a roundabout, unpredictable way. It made Lucinda realize that she didn't need magic. All she needed was courage.

(Well, it did also give her that super-awesome magical underwater breath, but mostly as a safety precaution, because Locker 37 was not a fan of drowning children.)

With her fear conquered, Lucinda decided not to hold her breath for minutes. Or hours. Or days. She emerged from the water after exactly fifty-nine seconds, the loser of the contest, but the winner of newfound confidence.

"So close!" Beatrice shouted as she jumped up and down at the edge of the pool. "But I win. Wow, that was an amazing contest!"

"Yeah," Lucinda said with a smile. "It sure was."

"And you don't have to give me your snacks," Beatrice said as she patted her friend on the back. "I've got too many snacks already. Do you still want some of mine?"

So it's a happy story, but what's the ultimate point of it?

Locker 37 trusted Lucinda to figure out things on her own.

It also trusted Riley.

Chapter Seventeen

SOMETHING RILEY FIGURED OUT

"**I** screwed up the vent fishing, in case that wasn't obvious," Original Riley told Red Riley, Blue Riley, and Orange Riley in the Dungeon. "But fishing got me thinking. Why do people fish?"

"So the world can have fish sticks!" Red Riley answered.

"Exactly," Riley said. "And what are fish sticks served on?"

Orange Riley thought things over for a moment, then smiled because she'd also figured out the new plan. "We're sneaking into the cafetorium, aren't we?"

"Yes," Riley said. "At least Orange Me and Red Me are."

"It's not lunchtime yet. And I don't think the fish sticks are—" Red Riley started to say, but Riley interrupted her.

"No eating," Riley explained. "You're gathering lunch trays. And, Blue Me"— she pointed at Blue Riley, who had thankfully followed her orders and remained in the Dungeon—"have a look at this."

Riley unrolled a large piece of paper with blue markings on it.

"What is it?" Blue Riley asked.

"The schematics of the heating ducts," Riley said.

"Oh yeah," Blue Riley said as she scratched her chin and looked up at nothing in particular. "From when I joined the Junior Janitor Club!"

The rest of the Rileys scratched their chins and looked up at nothing in particular, too.

This is a quick detour into the past.
Riley and all her clones were having the
same memory at the same time. It was from
the day before, so still fresh in their minds.
It involved the Junior Janitor Club.

For all of its history, the Junior Janitor
Club had been an exclusive club with a
single member: Keisha James. That is until
yesterday, when Riley begged Keisha to be
appointed the club's Master of Documents.

"How can I trust you to be a responsible
Master of Documents?" Keisha asked her.

And Riley said, "Maybe you can't,
because I'm dedicated to a life of mischief.
But I'm also dedicated to making sure
that the Junior Janitor Club finally gets the
recognition it deserves."

Keisha knew Riley's reputation for rule breaking. But she also knew that Riley was a master of public relations. That meant if Riley promised to spread the word about something, then the word would spread far and wide. Though it was usually not wise to ask Riley questions about her methods.

"I don't know if you remember, but you taught me to be bad once," Keisha said.

"I do remember," Riley said. "And did that work out for you?"

Keisha shrugged and said, "It took some time, but it eventually did."

"It always does."

Keisha took one more moment to think things over . . . then she handed Riley a set of keys. The set included a key to the filing cabinet in the janitor's office, where the schematics of the heating ducts were kept.

"If you get caught, then you will say you stole these from me," Keisha said. "And . . . ?"

"And what?"

"And you're really a member of the club now, which means you will have to participate in all club activities."

Riley shrugged and grabbed the keys.

FLASHBACK HAS NOW ENDED! WE REPEAT: FLASHBACK HAS NOW ENDED!

Back in the Dungeon, the Rileys stopped scratching their chins and stopped looking up at nothing in particular.

"I wonder what the club activities are," Orange Riley said. "Keisha never explained, did she?"

"Not my concern right now," Original Riley replied. "Right now, I want Blue Me to figure out the shortest path through the heating ducts from here to the gym."

"Got it," Blue Riley said as she looked closer at the schematics and pulled a Sharpie out of her pocket. "And I'm supposed to draw some lines so that Red Me and Orange Me can go into the heating ducts and know where to duct-tape the lunch trays, which will create a path for the Ping-Pong balls to travel directly to the gym."

"Um . . . how did you—?" Riley started to say.

"Know?" Blue Riley said as she marked up the schematics. "Because I'm sorta already . . . you . . . or me . . . or whatever

I am. We're thinking on the same wavelength."

It was a good point, and Riley turned to see what wavelength the other two clones were on. But instead of responding, they simply grabbed the schematics and headed for the door. They already knew what to do. Because they were also sorta her, or themselves, or whatever they were.

Chapter Eighteen
MEANWHILE . . .

With stacks of lunch trays under their arms, and greasy paper bags in their hands, Red Riley and Orange Riley tiptoed separately through empty halls. They met up again in Mrs. Rosenstein's room.

Mrs. Rosenstein didn't teach any health classes until after lunch, which meant her room was empty except for some Madagascar hissing cockroaches.

"Up for another cockroach rain?" Red Riley asked Orange Riley.

Orange Riley considered it and then said, "Artists don't repeat themselves."

"But that was . . . the other me," Red Riley said, "I'm my own person."

"True enough, but ten thousand Ping-Pong balls are so much more epic," Orange Riley said. "It'll be like a sequel to the cockroach rain. Bigger, bolder, with a higher budget."

"Yeah," Red Riley said as she opened the vent. "But only Original Me is going to get the credit."

Orange Riley sighed and shrugged. It was true. But what else could she do?

She could go on with the plan.

She and Red Riley fed the lunch trays into the heating duct and then climbed inside after them.

Meanwhile . . .

Blue Riley was reading graffiti on the walls of the Dungeon. It said:

Greta Hallowell Is Still Invisible.

Blue Riley had no idea who Greta Hallowell was or if she was still, in fact, invisible, but Blue Riley suddenly wondered why Locker 37 hadn't given the first Riley something to make her invisible.

Which made her wonder about Greta Hallowell again. Which made her nervous.

"Greta," she whispered. "Are you in here with me? If so, don't do anything.

Because that would be super scary."

Meanwhile . . .

Green Riley was still in front of the school, in a tree, in the middle of the playground. She was throwing acorns.

Which was . . . not the best choice.

Chapter Nineteen

THE BITHAWEST

The original Riley was pretending this was a regular day. She was in social studies, sitting next to Hunter Barnes.

Hunter was wearing a green headband that Riley hadn't noticed earlier. This worried her. Because if Hunter was wasting his time adding new accessories to his wardrobe, it meant he probably didn't do what she had asked him to do.

"Did you get it?" she asked.

He nodded.

"And it's ready to go?" she also asked.

He grinned a guilty grin.

"And you won't say a word to anyone?" she finally asked.

"Stop droning on and on," Hunter whispered. "As long as you keep your part of the deal, I'll keep mine."

At that moment, Kendall Ali stumbled into the classroom and slapped a tardy slip on Mrs. Shen's desk.

"Dentith," he mumbled as drool dripped down his chin. "Novocaine."

Mrs. Shen nodded sympathetically (she'd suffered through her own dentist appointment the week before), and she pointed to an empty seat behind Riley.

As Kendall sat down, he tapped Riley on the shoulder. "I juth thaw you outthide," he said.

"Wasn't me," Riley said as she pulled her hat over her face.

"I thaw you," Kendall said, his speech slurred because of the novocaine that had numbed his mouth. "In a twee. Hat wath gween. You thwew acowns at me."

Riley had forgotten that Green Riley was still outside, and it was obvious she was not doing as she was told (because no one told her to throw acorns at Kendall).

It wasn't surprising. Riley herself didn't always do what she was told.

"Oh, right," Riley said, acting like it was no big deal. "That was me. I'm good at multitasking."

Kendall's eyes narrowed in suspicion.

"I can back her up on that," Hunter said. "And Riley is so fast that she can literally be in two places at once."

"That's . . . bithawe," Kendall said, meaning to say "bizarre."

"She is the bithawest," Hunter said in a mocking tone, making fun of both Kendall and Riley at the same time.

It didn't work, though, because Riley took it as a compliment. She was totally in favor of being bizarre. It was nearly as good as being unpredictable.

"Thank you for saying so," Riley said, and out of instinct, she tipped her hat.

Oh.

No.

Taking her hat off meant that all her clones were frozen in place!

Red Riley and Orange Riley were hidden in the heating ducts, and Blue Riley was still in the Dungeon, so Riley wasn't too worried about them. Green Riley was her main concern. She was outside. Kendall had already seen her, so other people would see her, too, especially if she was frozen in place, in the act of throwing acorns at them.

But Riley couldn't unfreeze Green Riley by putting the hat back on. Because that would create a new clone, right in the middle of social studies!

A better solution was Finn and Gill.

Chapter Twenty
FINN AND GILL

The mascots for Mrs. Shen's classroom were the pair of goldfish that lived in a bowl in the back of the room. Keisha fed them every morning. The other kids always gave them warm greetings.

"What's bubblin', Finn?"

"Hope everything is going swimmingly, Gill."

And so on.

Keisha was very protective of Finn and Gill, especially since Hunter once dropped them down a drain in the Dungeon and they were never seen again. (Don't worry, it was in an alternate timeline.) But Riley needed to get at least one of them out of the bowl. Which would require some smooth moves. Luckily, Riley had them.

She raised her hand.

"Yes, Riley?" Mrs. Shen said.

"I've prepared something for the class," Riley said. "And I'd like to share it."

"Is it . . . appropriate?" Mrs. Shen asked, which was a valid question concerning anything Riley wanted to share.

"Totally," Riley said. "It's about last week's history lesson. You know, the twins who founded the city of Rome?"

"Romulus and Remus?" Mrs. Shen said. "That was mythology."

"Whatever it was, I've created an interpretive dance about it," Riley said. "It's called 'Romulus and Remus and Riley.' Check it out."

Riley then proceeded to spin and jump all about the room, swinging her rainbow hat around and grabbing everyone's attention. The dance obviously had nothing to do with Romulus or Remus or Rome or mythology. But it was a spectacular distraction.

"Captivating, Riley, but I don't see how this—" Mrs. Shen started to say, but her voice was overpowered by clapping.

Bryce was the ringleader. He was *really* into the dance. He was clapping out

an infectious beat for Riley to move to, and the entire class joined in.

As Riley danced by the fishbowl, she bumped it with her elbow, which sent Finn (or was it Gill?) flying out of the bowl and—*plop!*—into her hat.

Bingo!

Immediately, a clone fish popped into existence in the fishbowl. And sure enough, it was wearing a tiny green version of Riley's hat.

The plan was working perfectly.

Her dance was so distracting that no one had seen her bump the fish into the hat. The Riley clones were now unfrozen. And the only new clone that Riley had created was a tiny goldfish that looked exactly like the one that used to be in the bowl (and was now hidden in Riley's hat). The single difference was that the fish clone was wearing its own tiny hat.

Surely no one would notice that.

And at first, no one did notice. The class was still too focused on Riley's odd dance. Even Keisha wasn't keeping an eye on her little fishy friends.

Until Kendall, his mouth still numb from novocaine, shouted, "The fith!"

Riley stopped.

"Excuse me?" Mrs. Shen said.

"The fith! The fith!" Kendall shouted, waving his arms.

"The fifth what?" Mrs. Shen asked.

There was a hand signal that fourth-graders used for alerting other fourth-graders that the strange things they were witnessing were related to Locker 37. They would basically spread all ten of their fingers in front of their body.

Because 3 + 7 = 10. Obviously.

Riley wanted to keep her prank as secret as possible. At this point, only Carson, Bryce, and Hunter knew that something was up. And only Hunter knew the actual details. Still, she saw no choice but to flash Kendall the signal.

She set her rainbow hat on her desk and flashed all ten fingers at Kendall. His eyes widened in recognition.

"The fifth what?" Mrs. Shen asked again.

"The fifth grade isn't ready for my awe-inspiring interpretive dances," Riley said. "I should probably skip middle school entirely. Maybe even go straight to college. Or to

Broadway, where my talents would be appreciated."

Mrs. Shen rolled her eyes. "And I'm sure that's exactly what you meant to say, right, Kendall?"

Kendall, to Mrs. Shen's surprise, nodded. But he didn't say anything. He was too busy watching the fishbowl out of the corner of his eye.

Because there were now fifteen goldfish in it!

Riley quickly sat down with her rainbow hat in her lap. Gill (or was it Finn?) was flopping up and down in it, which meant he was taking the hat off and putting it on, over and over again.

He was creating and freezing multiple goldfish clones!

Chapter Twenty-One

THE MIRACLE OF LIFE

It was a good thing Riley had a full water bottle nearby.

It was also a good thing that her ridiculous and wonderful hat was waterproof.

Because when she emptied her water bottle into it, the hat didn't leak. And Finn (or was it Gill?) was soon safely swimming inside, not flopping around and creating a multitude of clones.

However, the fishbowl was now jam-packed with clones, each wearing a different-colored hat. As Mrs. Shen turned to the whiteboard to begin the social studies lesson, Riley turned to Keisha. There was no way to hide this strange new development, so she figured she'd get ahead of it.

"Finn and Gill must be in love," she whispered.

"Why?" Keisha whispered back.

"Because they started a family."

When Keisha turned to the bowl and saw what Riley was talking about, she didn't scream, or gasp, or get angry. She didn't question the lack of eggs, or any of the biology of the situation. She didn't even mention the hats! Which was not like Keisha at all.

She simply became a puddle of happiness. Because that's what happens to almost everybody when they love something so much.

"Oh my goodness gracious, will you look at that?" Keisha cooed as her body vibrated with joy. "We need to get you li'l darlin's into a bigger home."

Then she jumped up and grabbed the bowl. She hurried to the sink in the corner of the room, plugged the drain, turned on the tap, and turned the bowl over, dumping all the fish into the water.

"Keisha?" Mrs. Shen asked. "Is everything okay?"

"Better than okay," Keisha shouted.

"Gather round, class, and witness the miracle of life!"

The kids all rushed to the sink, with Mrs. Shen following, shaking her head, and saying, "Okay, what now?"

Riley grabbed Carson by the shoulder, preventing him from witnessing the miracle of life. "I need you to hide this for me until the end of class," she said, and she handed him the hat.

Water splashed over the sides and onto Carson's shirt.

"What the heck is wrong with you?" he said, pushing the hat back at her.

"My plan is spiraling out of control, so I need you to do this," she said, pushing it back to him, only this time she pushed too hard and Gill (or was it Finn?) flopped over the brim onto the floor.

"Now look what you've done," Carson said as he dove to the floor to scoop up the fish.

Since the fish was no longer in the hat, it meant all the clones froze in place.

"What are they doing?" Keisha said. "My sweet little babies aren't moving!"

"This one is," Carson announced as he rushed over to the sink with a wiggling Finn (or was it Gill?) in his cupped hands. He dropped the fish in with the others.

Riley was standing alone in the middle of the room with a hat full of water. No one was looking at her. They were all concentrating on the frozen fish.

"Oh well," she said with a sigh. Then she deposited the hat onto her head, which resulted in the following:

> 1. She got wet.
> 2. The clones, including all the clone fish, started moving again, which was a huge relief to Keisha and everyone else huddled over the sink.
> 3. A new clone of Riley, with a yellow hat, popped into existence.

"Nice to meet you, Yellow Me," Riley whispered. "Now get the heck to the utility room to monitor the furnace before it's too late."

Yellow Riley winked, straightened her yellow hat, and ran out the door.

Chapter Twenty-Two

UNFROZEN CLONES

Red Riley and Orange Riley peeled the last bits of duct tape off their legs. They wore the same clothes and accessories that Original Riley was wearing when she opened Locker 37, which meant they also had fishing rods and reels duct-taped to their legs.

They used the duct tape to attach the lunch trays to the heating ducts, blocking certain routes until they created one path from the Dungeon to the gym.

"I hate being frozen," Orange Riley said as she taped the last tray opposite the vent to the gym so that it redirected the balls and they had nowhere to go but down and out.

"Do you think we're the first person in history to use duct tape on an actual duct?" Red Riley asked Orange Riley.

"It's likely," Orange Riley said as she finished up the taping. "Can I be honest for a moment?"

"Of course! You're talking to me here."

"I've been thinking about movies where people are crawling around in heating ducts, and it seems super awesome, but it's actually kinda dangerous, isn't it?"

"Kinda? No, it's super dangerous. These could collapse at any moment. Not to mention the suffocation possibility. I would not recommend this to anyone, and especially not to impressionable children who might want to try this."

"I can't believe I even talked myself into this."

"I'm just glad I brought this as a reward for myself," Red Riley said as she held up a greasy paper bag.

Orange Riley smiled. "Yeah, I think it's okay to be selfish at this point."

Meanwhile . . .

Blue Riley was still in the Dungeon, and she was bored. So she was writing graffiti on the toilet stall with her Sharpie: *Blue Me Is the Best Me.*

Green Riley was still outside. She was no longer throwing acorns at people and was now trying to catch bumblebees with her fishing rod and reel. She wasn't having much luck.

And Yellow Riley was in the utility room. It had been Red Riley's job to monitor the furnace earlier, but she had abandoned her post to try her luck at vent fishing. It remained to be seen whether Yellow Riley would do the same. But one thing was for sure. Yellow Riley—or any Riley, for that matter—didn't fully understand how the furnace worked.

She knew that when the temperature dropped, the furnace was supposed to turn on and start blowing air through the ducts. She figured there might be a power button or a thermostat with temperature controls. But there were so many knobs and switches and dials that she didn't know where to start.

If the furnace turned on too early, she wasn't sure how to turn it off. And if it didn't turn on at the right moment, she didn't know how to make it go on.

Yellow Riley—or any Riley, for that matter—didn't like not knowing things.

So what did she do?

"Time to educate myself," she said to herself.

And she started pushing and twisting and pulling almost anything that could be pushed or twisted or pulled.

Chapter Twenty-Three
WHOOSH!

*W*hoosh!

Blue Riley heard it first.

(Actually, Yellow Riley heard it first, but she was the one who caused it, so she doesn't count.)

The *whoosh* was followed by *bumpity bumpity bumpity*!

But it was more like tens of thousands of bumpities.

Blue Riley dropped her Sharpie and ran to the vent in the Dungeon. Hot air was blasting through the vent, but she was still able to pull it open.

She held her blue hat tight to her hair and stuck her head inside. As the hot air blasted past her, she looked down the dark tunnel of heating ducts.

The ten thousand Ping-Pong balls were gone. They were already on their way toward the gym.

Oh.

No.

Chapter Twenty-Four

THE "HOW RILEY GOT 10,000 PING-PONG BALLS" CHAPTER

Warning: *There's arithmetic in this chapter. Feel free to check the calculations, but that would be a waste of your time. They're perfect.*

A quick question for you: Where's the first place you'd look to buy a bunch of Ping-Pong balls?

Unless your town is home to a Ping-Pong ball factory, there's a good chance you'd check the Internet, right? Perhaps Amazon.com? (Though you really should be supporting your local mom-and-pop Ping-Pong ball retailers whenever possible.)

- According to Riley's research, she could get 100 Ping-Pong balls on Amazon for about $10. That was 10 cents per Ping-Pong ball.

- Not bad, but 10,000 balls at that rate still cost $1,000, even with free shipping. And Riley didn't have that kind of cash.

- She did a little more digging and she found that Alibaba.com, the Chinese equivalent of Amazon, listed a Ping-Pong ball manufacturer that would sell her 10,000 Ping-Pong balls for only $250. If you're good with fractions, you know that's 1/4 the cost of Amazon.

Now we're talking! Still a hefty sum for a

fourth-grader, but surely Riley could come up with it. She did have a piggy bank and a $5/week allowance, after all.

But wait . . .

Alibaba.com didn't offer free shipping. And remember, these Ping-Pong balls were all the way over in China. Riley didn't want to pay standard shipping and wait for her Ping-Pong balls to be packed into crates, then into shipping containers, which would go on trucks, and then be loaded onto freight trains, and then lifted onto a boat that would *putt-putt-putt* its way across the Pacific Ocean, then back onto freight trains, and so on, until they arrived at her door.

That would take months!

She wanted those Ping-Pong balls in a day or two.

- Well, according to that one particular Ping-Pong ball manufacturer Riley found on Alibaba.com, 10,000 Ping-Pong balls cost only $250, but the express shipping for them ran about . . .

- $50,765,540.46.

- Yes, that's . . .

- **Fifty million . . .**
- **Seven hundred sixty-five thousand . . .**
- **Five hundred forty . . .**
- **Dollars!**
- **(Not to mention forty-six cents.)**

Now, you'd be right to guess that Riley's piggy bank didn't have even close to 50 million dollars in it. You'd also be right to guess that this shipping quote was probably the result of artificial intelligence gone awry. Because obviously it was an absurd amount of money to charge for sending Ping-Pong balls . . . anywhere.

- **Especially when you consider that they weighed only 2.7 grams apiece.**

- That meant that 10,000 Ping-Pong balls weighed 27,000 grams . . . which was 27 kilograms . . . which was only about 60 pounds . . . which was about the average weight of a third-grader.

- Surely Riley could've shipped a third-grader for less than 50 million dollars, right?

- In fact, a round-trip economy-class plane ticket from Beijing, China, to New York, New York, was available for $500 or less. And it would transport a third-grader between the two cities in less than 24 hours.

- That meant that if Riley had $50,765,540.46, she could've sent 101,531 third-graders to the United States from China . . . and then back home again.

- Or, for that matter, she could've bought
  10 round-trip plane tickets for each of her
  10,000 Ping-Pong balls (assuming they
  weren't fancy Ping-Pong balls
  who insisted on flying
  business class).

But clearly, Riley didn't get her Ping-Pong balls that way. So how did she get them?

Remember in the beginning of the chapter, where it said, "Unless your town is home to a Ping-Pong ball factory . . ."?

Well, Riley's town was home to a Ping-Pong ball factory: Paul Paulson's Ping-Pong Production Plant!

And Paul Paulson was done with the Ping-

Pong business. His Ping-Pong production plant was closing up shop. And since shipping Ping-Pong balls can be expensive for anyone other than Amazon.com (you're essentially shipping air), it made sense for Paul to unload his remaining inventory locally.

So a local mom-and-pop store, Mark and Martha's Miscellaneous Merchandise, bought all the Ping-Pong balls. And then Riley bought the 10,000 Ping-Pong balls from Mark and Martha for the low, low price of $100 (or 1 cent per ball), which was 20 weeks of her $5/week allowance that she had saved in her piggy bank.

- **Finally, just in case you're wondering, to get the $50,765,540.46 that the Chinese manufacturer was charging for express** shipping, Riley would've needed to save her $5/week allowance for 10,153,108 weeks (and 1 more day to get those 46 cents). That's just over 195,252 years.

- And that's only for the shipping. Add another year onto that to save the $250 to buy the actual Ping-Pong balls.

- She'd also need a really big piggy bank.

Chapter Twenty-Five

AN EARLY LUNCH

*W*hoosh ...

Bumpity bumpity bumpity ...

The original, and still slightly damp, Riley was in language arts when she heard the balls bumping through the ducts above. It sounded like a stampede of chipmunks.

Everyone else looked at the ceiling, but she looked at Hunter.

"Not my fault," he said as he pushed his hair out of his face and tucked it up into his green headband.

Outside, Green Riley was still hot on the trail of some bumblebees, running around the playground with her fishing rod and reel. But even she could hear the racket.

Is the prank happening already? she thought. *Am I missing it?*

She dropped the rod and ran toward the nearest entrance to the school.

Back in the heating ducts, Red Riley and Orange Riley were treating themselves to an early lunch. They'd finished the job of creating the perfect tunnel for the Ping-Pong balls. Now they were digging into their greasy paper bags and pulling out some fish sticks.

And where on earth did they get fish sticks?

From the cafetorium, of course, the one place in the school where there's a convection oven and some very industrious lunch ladies.

Did you think they grabbed only trays while they were there? Silly you. These are Rileys we're talking about, the school's biggest fish stick aficionados.

"What's that sound?" Red Riley asked as she raised a fish stick toward her mouth and stopped.

"I don't know, but do you feel warm?" Orange Riley replied as she, too, raised a fish stick and stopped.

Then they saw the first one.

A single Ping-Pong ball was faster

than the rest. It arrived alone, bouncing through the heating duct toward them as if it were a happy little bird.

"Aw, look at that," they both said at the same time.

The screaming started about a second later, when the rest of the balls burst through the heating duct and knocked the fish sticks into Red and Orange Riley's faces.

"Holy baked manicotti!" they hollered as they were caught in a torrent of white.

Ever watch a lottery drawing on TV? Where a bunch of balls with numbers on them bounce and tumble around?

It was sort of like that. Only with two Rileys stuck in the middle of the balls, screaming. Plus, no one was going to win any money.

Chapter Twenty-Six
REGROUPING

Whoosh . . .

  Bumpity bumpity bumpity . . .

Footsteps!

Yellow Riley heard them coming down the stairs into the utility room. She scampered to a corner and hid behind a stack of boxes.

"What is this nonsense?!" shouted Reggie Blue, the school janitor, as he rushed over to the furnace.

Yellow Riley watched as Reggie readjusted some of the knobs and dials she had turned, and she took a mental note of what he did.

Immediately, the furnace turned off.

"Keisha wouldn't have done this," Reggie said to himself as he scratched his head and walked up the stairs. "So who?"

As soon as he was gone, Yellow Riley slipped out of her hiding place.

"Me, that's who," she said as she studied the knobs and dials and remembered the adjustments Reggie had made. "And next time I'll do it right."

Meanwhile . . .

Over in the ducts above the gym, Red Riley and Orange Riley were now red and orange. Literally.

Being pelted by thousands of flying Ping-Pong balls will do that to your skin.

Since all the vents were still closed, the Ping-Pong balls had nowhere to go except to pummel the two Rileys.

But when Reggie turned off the heat, the balls settled, and Red Riley and Orange Riley were able to push them away.

To give the balls an escape route, the two Rileys finally wiggled the vent above the gym from the inside. It fell open. The next time the heat went on, those balls would be erupting from the gym ceiling.

Success! Their job was officially done.

They collected their hats and crawled out of the other vent and back into Mrs. Rosenstein's room.

The bell for the lunch period was about to ring, and Mrs. Rosenstein would soon arrive. They knew they had to find somewhere else to hide. So Red Riley and Orange Riley got moving.

Around the same time, Blue Riley backed away from the vent in the Dungeon. That's when the door opened and Green Riley ran in.

"Is everything under control?" Green Riley asked. "I didn't miss it, did I?"

"I think it's okay," Blue Riley said.

"So what's next?" Green Riley asked.

"Waiting is next," Original Riley said as she entered the Dungeon. "It's lunchtime, and I need the rest of me to hang out down here. I'm on my way to the cafetorium to talk to Carson."

"Don't count on any fish sticks being there," Orange Riley told her as she and Red Riley stumbled into the Dungeon. Their hair was wilder than ever, and their skin was still discolored from all the Ping-Pong balls and fish sticks that had smashed against it.

"Cleaned the cafetorium out of the last ones," Red Riley explained.

Riley glared at herselves for a moment.

"Maybe next time don't ask me to do something that's so dangerous, and maybe then there will be some fish sticks left over," Orange Riley said with a smirk.

"Yeah, maybe next time send Dad's drone to do the dirty work instead," Red Riley said with a bigger smirk.

From all that smirking, Original Riley

could tell the clones were upset. And yet this seemed like an unfair criticism. She had only asked them to do what she was willing to do herself. She was about to say exactly that when—

"Sorry for the whole furnace whoopsie-daisy," Yellow Riley said as she busted into the Dungeon, nearly out of breath. "I have it under control now."

"Who's that?" the other clones asked. "Is she a new me?"

"I'm the *newest* me," Yellow Riley said.

"Yep, she's me, all right," Original Riley said. "And now that everyone is acquainted, stay here. Where it's safe. I'm talking to all of me. And I mean it!"

Chapter Twenty-Seven

THE ROBOT REBELLION IS UPON US

Riley placed her tray of spaghetti on a table in the cafetorium and sat down next to Carson. She sighed a big sigh.

"Hey, dude," she said. "A day without fish sticks is a day without—"

"Sunshine," Carson said, finishing her sentence. "Please stop."

"Stop what?"

"You're so—"

"Don't say it. Don't call me predictable."

"But you are," Carson said. "I knew you were going to complain about fish sticks the moment you walked in here. And now I know what you're going to do next. I'll show you. Gimme your Sharpie."

"How did you know I have a Sharpie?"

"You always have a Sharpie."

"That's true, but that hardly makes me predictable," Riley said as she pulled the Sharpie out of her pocket and handed it to Carson. "That makes me prepared."

Carson proceeded to jot something down on his paper napkin.

"There's no way you know what I'll do next," Riley went on. "I'm a conductor of chaos, a maestro of misdirection. If I were a knight, my name would be Riley the Random. And you would be my loyal page. And as luck would have it, loyal page, I have a quest for you. It's a quest that's so random, it'll hardly feel like a quest at all. What you have to do is borrow two Roombas from the—"

Carson set the Sharpie down and put his hand up to cut Riley off. Then he slid the napkin over so she could see what he had written.

You're going to order me to do something stupid, and dangerous, and possibly illegal.

Riley scrunched up her face. "But it'll be fun."

"For you, maybe," Carson said, and he picked up his lunch and walked away to another table.

A few minutes later, Riley was back in the Dungeon, and the clones were huddled around her.

"All I wanted Carson to do was borrow two Roombas from the janitor's closet," she said. "And then all he had to do after that was strap them to his feet and ride them through the halls, screaming, 'Help! Help! The robot rebellion is upon us! The robot rebellion is upon us!' Was that so much to ask?"

"And remind me again why I needed him to do this?" Red Riley asked.

Orange Riley stuck a finger up in recognition and said, "It's always good to set up another suspect to blame for your prank."

"But robots?" Yellow Riley said.

"The perfect scapegoats," Blue Riley replied. "It's impossible to feel guilty if robots take the blame."

"But if it didn't work, Carson would take the blame," Green Riley said. "So why not use Hunter instead?"

"Because Hunter already has a job," Original Riley said. "Speaking of which, I have to help him."

The clones groaned.

"I promised," Riley said. "And I keep my promises. Plus, there's time. Everything is set, right? The balls are in place and the vent is open, right?"

Red Riley and Orange Riley nodded

as they rubbed
the sore spots
on their bodies
and made nasty
faces at Yellow Riley.

"And now I know how to turn the heat
on and off," Yellow Riley told them.

"Good," Original Riley said. "Yellow Me
will go back to the utility room, and when
the signal sounds, the furnace will go on."

Yellow Riley flashed her a thumbs-up.

"Which means the prank is ready,
ready, ready," Riley said.

The clones looked at one another,
shrugged, and nodded.

"Great," Riley said. "So it's time to help
Hunter. Go find some aprons. As for me,
I'm going to class. Wish me luck."

Chapter Twenty-Eight
NERVES

Riley needed luck because math class made her nervous.

Not because she was bad at math (she knew how to calculate shipping rates for Ping-Pong balls, after all), but because the prank was ready and it was only the fifth period of the day. There was still recess and Spanish before the assembly, and Riley wasn't sure she could contain her excitement. She could hardly keep herself in her seat. She kept wiggling and fidgeting.

"Is everything okay?" Mrs. Shen asked Riley.

"I'm . . . bouncing along fine," Riley said.

"Okay, then bounce your attention to the whiteboard," Mrs. Shen said, "as we work on the candy graph. You're the only one who hasn't told us what your favorite candy is."

"Oh yeah, right," Riley said.

"Looks like we have six kids who love Skittles," Mrs. Shen said. "Six for gummy bears. Four for Reese's Peanut Butter Cups. Three for Sour Patch Kids. And one for . . . black licorice."

Carson was watching Riley, and when

she turned to look at him, he turned away. He was the only kid who voted for black licorice, and while that was nothing to be embarrassed about, it clearly embarrassed him.

"Skittles better win it," Keisha said. "Break the tie, Riley. Break the tie!"

"No, go for gummy bears, gummy bears, gummy bears!" Bryce chanted.

"This isn't a competition," Mrs. Shen said. "It's simply a poll. And we're graphing the results."

Riley didn't like candy, so theoretically, she could've chosen anything. Of course, she knew that it would make Carson feel better if she chose black licorice. But that also wouldn't be authentic. It wouldn't be unique, and Riley wanted to be unique.

"Fish sticks," she finally said.

Mrs. Shen flinched at the suggestion, and various kids in the class said, "Eww!"

"Fish sticks are not candy," Keisha told Riley.

"I have to agree with Keisha on this one," Mrs. Shen said. "Fish and candy don't mix. At all."

"But they're my favorite treat," Riley said. "So please put them on the graph."

Mrs. Shen shrugged and added fish sticks to the whiteboard.

Carson sighed, and then raised his hand. "Can I go to the bathroom, please?"

Mrs. Shen nodded and Carson stood. As he walked past Riley, she grabbed his sleeve. "Stay out of the Dungeon, please," she whispered.

He pulled his arm away and didn't answer. He didn't even look back as he headed out the door. And that made Riley nervous, too.

When recess rolled around, Riley was even more nervous. She paced back and forth and constantly asked her classmates and recess monitors what time it was.

"It's high time for you to participate in an official Junior Janitor Club activity," Keisha said when Riley asked her. "And to get the club the recognition it deserves. Like you promised."

"Of course," Riley replied, though she had forgotten her promise to Keisha. "So what exactly does a Junior Janitor Club activity entail?"

"Since you're the Master of Documents, I want you to draft an inventory of all the trash cans in the school," Keisha said.

"Draft a what?"

"I want you to create a document telling me the number and location of every trash can in school. And we'll analyze the most efficient way to empty them after school."

"And why would we do that?"

"Because that's the sort of thing Junior Janitor Club does," Keisha said with a hand over her heart. "This isn't about bake sales, buddy. It's about making a difference. Reggie Blue is overworked and underpaid and he needs our help to keep the school in tip-top shape."

"Yeah, but what about, like, child labor laws?" Riley said.

Keisha rolled her eyes. "We're volunteering to do this. And now I'm regretting ever giving you those keys."

A promise was a promise, and Riley was determined to keep hers. Even if it made her nerves feel more . . . nervous.

"Don't worry," Riley said to Keisha (but also to herself). "I've still got time to make the club proud. And I will."

Chapter Twenty-Nine

TARTA DE CEBOLLA

Riley's sigh echoed through the Dungeon.

"There's one more job," she told the clones, who were all wearing aprons and covered in flour. "It means missing the big finale, though."

The clones' eyes were all red and watery, which looked especially sad under the Dungeon's flickering lights.

"This was always a possibility," Riley reminded them. "Because it would be too suspicious to have a bunch of me hanging around the gym during the big moment. It might ruin everything. Plus, there's one last promise to keep."

The clones wiped tears from their faces with their sleeves, and they nodded.

"At least *I'll* be able to watch it," Riley said. "So it's sort of like all of me will get to see it."

This was stretching the truth, and Riley couldn't bear to see the looks of disappointment on the clones' faces. But those looks quickly changed, even before Riley had a chance to turn away.

It happened the moment Red Riley picked up a large paper bag and held

it out. The sad looks transformed into proud looks.

"This is for the other promise," Red Riley said.

"Really?" Original Riley asked as she took the bag, which had steam coming out of it. "That fast?"

"The cafetorium's convection oven cooks things so fast, it might as well be a time-travel machine," Red Riley said.

Original Riley looked inside the bag and smiled. "No one saw you, right?"

"Especially not Hunter's mom," Red Riley assured her.

Hunter's mom worked in the cafetorium and was one of the nicest people in the school. Too bad the same couldn't be said about her son. But Riley had made a deal with Hunter, and thanks to her clones, she had kept up her end of it. So now it was time to see if he had kept up his.

Riley hurried to class, carefully carrying the steaming bag.

As she passed by other students in the hall, they said things like "What smells?" and "Something stinks!" and "Aughhh, gross."

Riley didn't respond. She kept moving until she was in Spanish class and she was sliding the bag underneath Hunter's desk.

Hunter sniffed the air and asked, "Is that what I think it is?"

"Your tarta de cebolla," Riley said. "For the cumpleaños de tu madre."

"My what what what?" Hunter asked. "For my what what what?"

"You really need to pay more attention in this class," Riley said as she pulled her Spanish book out of her backpack.

Hunter shrugged and looked in the bag. Then he smiled a wide smile.

"So, are we set?" Riley asked Hunter.

"Oh, boy, are we set," he responded. "Just you wait and see."

The way he said it worried Riley, though there was little she could do about anything now. The assembly was next period. She was at the "show must go on" stage of the prank.

"Hola, estudiantes," the Spanish teacher, Mrs. Diaz, said to announce the beginning of class.

"Hola, Señora Diaz," the students replied.

And Riley whispered, "Hola, mi amigo," as Carson sat at the desk in front of her.

Carson had been grumpy all day, and she didn't understand it. She wondered if the prank might cheer him up. Maybe the kindest thing to do was to give him the best view of it. A front-row seat, in other words.

But then she thought a little deeper about the situation.

Really thought.

She tried to put herself into her best

friend's shoes for a moment.

It was then that she realized how silly her idea for cheering him up was.

The entire day, Carson had basically told her how little interest he had in her prank. And the prank was inspired by proving Carson wrong. Giving him a front-row seat was the last thing that would help him.

But what *would* help him?

"I don't know how to say this in Spanish, but can you meet me on the way to the gym for the assembly?" she whispered. "I need to talk to you."

"Adiós" was all that Carson whispered back, and he didn't even turn around to look at her.

Chapter Thirty

BEST FRIENDS, PART 2

"What's going on?" Riley said, placing a hand on Carson's shoulder as he walked out of the classroom.

Carson stopped, turned, and scowled. "I should ask you the same thing."

"What do you mean?" Riley said.

Carson was so upset that he was trembling, and he started holding up fingers as he listed things off. "First, you and Bryce ruined parachute day. Then you joined Keisha's weird janitor club when you won't even support my love of black licorice. And now? Now you're giving stinky gifts to Hunter in Spanish."

"That's all part of—" Riley started to say, but Carson cut her off.

"What about me?" he said. "I'm supposed to be your best friend, when all you do is bark orders at me. 'Open a bunch of vents, Carson! Hide this ugly wet fish hat, Carson! Borrow some Roombas and . . .' Well, I can usually predict what you're going to do, but who knows what you wanted me to do with some Roombas."

Riley lowered her head and muttered, "Strap 'em to your feet and scream about the robot rebellion."

"Of course, the robot rebellion, I should've known," Carson said, and then he sniffled. "Because what else are best friends for?"

"Holy pumpkin ravioli with brown butter sauce . . . ," Riley whispered as her throat tightened and she lowered her head.

"All you think about is yourself and getting attention for yourself," Carson told her. "It's always about Riley, Riley, Riley."

This comment hit Riley harder than Carson could possibly realize. Maybe that's because there were literally five other Rileys who were sneaking through the school at that very moment. They were making maps of all the trash cans, emptying those trash cans, and leaving behind signs that said: JUNIOR JANITOR CLUB, WE'RE UBIQUITOUS!

(Ubiquitous means "everywhere," but chances are you knew that already, because you're very smart.)

Riley wanted to say that her clones

were doing this entirely out of generosity. After all, they were helping Keisha and the Junior Janitor Club. But she was beginning to understand that wasn't even close to true. Sure, she was keeping a promise, but it was a promise she made so that she could pull off her legendary prank.

It was indeed about Riley, Riley, Riley.

At that moment, she knew how right Carson was. Also how hurt he was. And she felt sad in a way she couldn't fully describe. It had nothing to do with herself, and everything to do with her best friend.

As their classmates all hurried toward the gym for the assembly, Riley and Carson remained in the hall. Their heads were hanging. They weren't looking at each other.

"I have to tell you something," Riley said.

"That you're going to be late for your prank," Carson replied.

"No," Riley said as she raised her head. "I have to tell you that I've been selfish. That I haven't been treating you like a best friend should be treated. Like anyone should be treated."

Carson raised his head, too. "Do you mean that?"

Riley nodded. "And I'd like to prove it to you."

"You're going to tell me where to sit to get the best view of your prank, right?" Carson said. "A front-row seat, in other words."

Riley put an arm around him and said, "No, that would be too predictable."

"Okay, then what are you going to tell me to do for you?"

"Nothing," Riley said. "I want to do whatever it is you want to do."

"I guess I want to . . . see your prank?" Carson said, though he was asking it more than saying it.

"Really?"

Carson thought about it for a second, then shook his head.

"Then we'll hang out here until you figure out what you really want," Riley said.

It meant that she'd miss the assembly and the prank, and while that would've been unthinkable to Riley earlier in the day, she now knew it was the best thing to do. Because it got rid of that sad feeling and replaced it with a new feeling.

The new feeling was best described as a good feeling. Maybe even a better feeling than Riley got from pulling off a prank. It seemed impossible, but it was true.

"Actually, do you know what I want?" Carson said.

"What?" Riley asked.

"To know where that music is coming from . . . and what's making that weird sound."

That's when Riley heard it, too: music coming from the announcement system, and a low, weird humming sound in the distance.

Chapter Thirty-One

THAT MUSIC AND THAT LOW, WEIRD HUMMING SOUND

To understand the music and the low, weird humming sound, we first have to recall the moment when Hunter caught Riley and her clones on the stairway down to the Dungeon.

Remember how there were tears running down his cheeks?

Hunter claimed it was because he was "cuttin' onions" when in reality he was . . .

well, he was actually, really, truly cutting onions. Who would've guessed?

You see, it was Hunter's mom's birthday that day, and he wanted to bake her a cake. The problem was, she didn't like cake. What she did like were onion tarts. Loved them, in fact. So Hunter decided to bake her an onion tart.

He had spent the morning cutting onions, and if you've ever cut onions, you know they can make your eyes water. He'd only cut two, and there were a lot more onions to cut and a lot more baking to do. As much as he wanted to give his mom the onion tart for her birthday, it would've been impossible for him to do it alone.

That's where Riley and the clones came in.

When Hunter stumbled upon all of Riley's clones, they needed him to stay quiet. So they agreed to help him. They promised to finish the onion tart for his mother's birthday. And that's exactly what they did.

They cut more onions.

They mixed the ingredients.

They slipped into the kitchen and popped the mixture into that miraculously fast convection oven.

Then Riley delivered the hot onion tart (or the tarta de cebolla, as it's called en español) to Hunter in Spanish class.

In return, Hunter agreed to keep quiet about the clones and to help them with the prank.

And he did keep quiet.

And he did help them with the prank.

And you're probably thinking, *This terrible author! He made me wait an entire book to reveal a secret about an . . . onion tart? An onion tart! Are you kidding me?*

Yes.

And no.

You see, Hunter also did something else.

But you already know what that is, because you picked up on the foreshadowing, right?

Chapter Thirty-Two

FLASHBACK ALERT!

FLASHBACK ALERT! FLASHBACK ALERT! FLASHBACK ALERT!

This is another quick detour into the past, revisiting that moment in the Dungeon when Riley asked Hunter to do something, which you weren't allowed to hear about until now (because it made for better storytelling, or something like that).

"This is what we need you to do," Riley said to Hunter in the Dungeon. "My house is a quick walk from school. There's a shed

in the backyard that's unlocked. My dad
works on projects in it and he has a little
boom box—"

"A what box?" Hunter asked.

"A boom box," Orange Riley said. "It's
like a giant ancient cell phone, but you
can't get the Internet or call anyone or do
much of anything with it. Just music."

"Classical music," Blue Riley added.
"Dad loves classical music."

"Go get the boom box and hook it up to
the announcement system," Red Riley said.
"You'll play some classical music during
last period to accompany the prank."

"Pranks are always better with musical
accompaniment," Green Riley said.

"Especially classical music," Original
Riley said. "It makes it . . . classier."

Hunter nodded and smiled and said, "I can handle that."

FLASHBACK HAS NOW ENDED! WE REPEAT: FLASHBACK HAS NOW— WAIT. NO. THERE'S STILL SOME MORE FLASHING BACK TO DO, BECAUSE THIS IS ACTUALLY HUNTER'S FLASHBACK AND NOT RILEY'S FLASHBACK. SORRY ABOUT THAT. PLEASE BE ADVISED THAT WE'RE STILL FLASHING BACK! STILL FLASHING BACK! STILL FLASHING BACK!

Hunter slipped out of the Dungeon, but he didn't go to Riley's house. Instead, he went to the gym locker room. He was the first kid there, so no one noticed when he pulled a piece of rainbow-colored fabric out of his pocket.

And definitely no one noticed when he took that piece of rainbow-colored fabric and tied it around his head like a headband

and created a clone of himself.

"Hold up," you're probably saying to yourself. "HE DID WHAT?"

He created a clone of himself. Was that not clear?

Okay, fine. This might require some explaining.

But rather than confusing things further by issuing a Flashback Within a Flashback Alert! we're simply going to ask you to turn back to Chapter Nine: Cuttin' Onions. We'll wait here, in the middle of this flashback, while you read it.

Waiting . . .

Waiting . . .

Waiting . . .

Done? Good.

Remember the part where Hunter pulled

on Riley's hat? Well, at that moment, he ripped off one of the hat's multiple rainbow-colored ribbons. Then he hid it in his pocket. Riley and her clones never even noticed! (But you probably did.)

It helps to know that pieces of Locker 37's magical objects will often work equally as well as the entire object. For instance, if a kid had a magic eraser and broke it into pieces, each piece would erase things. But that's another story.

This story is about how Hunter acquired a rainbow-colored headband that made clones.

You might have noticed Hunter was wearing a headband in Chapter Nineteen: The Bithawest (feel free to read that chapter again, too—it's an amusing one).

You might have also noticed that the headband was green, not rainbow colored.

"That's some terrible editing by this book's publishing company," you're probably saying to yourself.

But you'd be wrong. This book's publishing company is infallible (infallible means they make no mistakkes).

Because, you see, the kid wearing the headband wasn't Hunter.

He was his clone!

Hunter created his green-headband-wearing clone that morning in the gym locker room, as soon as he put on the rainbow-colored headband.

And he told his green-headband-wearing clone, "Go to class for me. And try not to get into too much trouble."

Green Hunter shrugged, which was his way of saying yes, and that left Original Hunter free to go wherever and do whatever he wanted, without any consequences.

And you know what?

Original Hunter went exactly where Riley asked him to go, and did exactly what she asked him to do.

He walked to her house and went into her shed and got her dad's boom box, and he hooked the boom box up to the announcement system so that it would play classical music while the Ping-Pong balls shot from the gym ceiling and therefore make the prank classier.

But that's not all that Hunter did.

Because he also found something other than a boom box in the shed, something else that was owned by Riley's dad, something he could clone . . .

FLASHBACK HAS NOW ENDED! WE REPEAT: FLASHBACK HAS NOW ENDED! AND WE MEAN IT THIS TIME.

Chapter Thirty-Three

ONE HUNDRED CLONE . . .

The music Carson and Riley heard in the hall was, you guessed it, classical music. It was coming out of the announcement system. It was the beginning of a symphony called *Thus Spoke Zarathustra* and it went like this:

Dun . . .

Duuun . . .

Duuuuuun . . .

Dun dun!

You may have even heard it before. It's classy classical music, the type of thing that makes a prank so much better. And it proved to Riley that Hunter had kept his end of the deal.

Most of the students and teachers (except for Riley, Carson, and a few other stragglers) were in the gym by now, ready to watch the jugglers. To the audience, it probably seemed like the music was part of the jugglers' act.

But then there was that low, weird humming sound . . .

It was getting louder and louder and louder, as if a bunch of insects were racing down the hall toward Riley and Carson. It was ominous, to say the least, and Riley and Carson braced themselves for whatever it was.

But before whatever it was arrived, someone else did.

"The wobot webellion is upon us! The wobot webellion is upon us!"

A genuinely terrified Kendall Ali came running around the corner and down the hall past them, waving his arms as he went. He raced toward the gym . . . and he was being followed.

Five drones, their propellers humming, turned the corner next.

They were followed by five more.

Then ten more.

In seconds, the hall was full of humming drones. Everywhere. And each had a slightly different colored headband tied around it.

One hundred clone drones.

The sound of their humming was now nearly deafening, but there were two more sounds mixed in as well. Because when the music started, that was the signal to Yellow Riley, who was waiting in the utility room to turn on the furnace.

So there was a *whoosh* . . .

And a *bumpity bumpity bumpity* . . .

"Holy bigoli," Riley said as she and Carson dove to the floor and the clone drones flew over them in a humming black stream. "I think I might actually get in big trouble for this."

"Actually, I think you might not be the one who's getting in big trouble," Carson said as he pointed up at the drones.

There, attached to the drones' colored headbands, were small banners that proved his point. They were like the ones that wave behind small airplanes as they fly over the beach. They all read:

YOU HAVE HUNTER BARNES TO THANK . . .
FOR HOPEWELL ELEMENTARY'S GREATEST
PRANK!

As the last of the drones passed over her and flew around the corner and into the gym, Riley jumped to her feet.

"Wait a second," she said to Carson. "Hunter is telling them that he did? I worked so hard for this. I . . . I . . . I . . ."

"You're speechless for once?" Carson said. "Maybe that's a good thing."

"But I went through so much. And now he gets the credit?" she said with a gasp.

"He also gets the blame," Carson replied. "He can be your scapegoat."

"And I'm absolutely fine with that," a voice from behind them said. "Scapegoat me all you want."

They turned around to see Hunter, the original Hunter, wearing his rainbow-colored headband and smiling widely.

"Holy spaghetti tacos," Riley said. "What did you do, Hunter?"

"Oh, nothing," he said. "Just made one hundred clones of your dad's drone, using this piece of your awesome cloning hat."

He tapped on his rainbow headband.

"But ... but ... but ... who's controlling all the drones?" Carson asked.

Somehow, Hunter's smile got wider, and he said, "You know what's better than one Hunter?"

That's when Riley realized that the Hunter she'd seen in class, the one with the green headband, was a clone.

"Two Hunters?" she asked.

"How about one hundred Hunters?" he said with a laugh. "See you around, dopes. I'm gonna go watch *my* prank now."

Then he ran toward the gym . . .

Where the music was blasting (*Dun . . . duuun . . . duuuuuun . . . dun dun!*) . . .

The clone drones were humming . . .

The heat was whooshing . . .

And the Ping-Pong balls were going *bumpity bumpity* until they started to shoot out from the ceiling.

Chapter Thirty-Four

HOPEWELL ELEMENTARY'S GREATEST PRANK

Even though they were still in the hall, Riley and Carson could figure out what was happening in the gym thanks to the chaos of voices they could hear coming from within.

"Gah! Drone swarm! Drone swarm!"

"Wah! Ping-Pong ball storm! Ping-Pong ball storm!"

"Wait! Are the Ping-Pong

balls bouncing off the drones?"

"I'm not sure if this is educational."

"Look at the jugglers! They're still going! That's too many balls for humans to juggle! It makes no sense!"

"Worst assembly ever!"

"Best assembly ever!"

"Why would drones wear headbands? It makes no sense!"

"Notice the complex physics at play, children. Very educational!"

"Look at all the sea turtle eggs!"

"You call Ping-Pong balls 'sea turtle eggs,' too?"

"Of course. Everybody does."

"How are the jugglers juggling so many sea turtle eggs? And now Sarah Abramson has joined the jugglers! She's better than they are. It makes no sense!"

"Did two fishing rods and reels just fly outta there, too?"

"Did I just get hit by a fish stick?"

"Okay, the fishing rods and fish sticks were too much, even for Sarah. She and the jugglers have collapsed. That actually makes sense."

"Who did this?"

"Hunter did this! It says so right there."

"Thank you, Hunter!"

"We hate you, Hunter!"

"Oh no, what about the drones? The jugglers are still down. Are they safe from the drones? I can't watch! It makes—"

"The wobot webellion is upon us! The wobot webellion is upon us! The wobot webellion is upon . . ."

Chapter Thirty-Five

PREDICTABLE

While there was still time to go in and see the glorious end of the prank before everyone started rushing out of the gym, Riley decided she wanted to go somewhere else.

"Come with me," she said, and she grabbed Carson's hand.

She led him down to the Dungeon, where they found the Blue, Green, Red,

Orange, and Yellow Rileys sitting with their backs against the wall. They all looked exhausted.

"Carson, meet . . . me," Riley said.

"Hey, Carson," all the clones said at the same time, and they flashed him the Locker 37 sign with their fingers.

"Okay . . . ," Carson said, nodding slowly. "Now I think I see what's going on."

Green Riley stood up, walked over to the original Riley, and put a hand on her shoulder. "I did everything I was supposed to do."

"The prank," Blue Riley said.

"The onion tart," Red Riley said.

"The trash cans," Orange Riley said.

"Everything," Yellow Riley said.

Original Riley nodded, then she said, "And I'm sorry about that. I've been so focused on myself and getting attention for myself that I didn't think about others. Like all of you. Like Carson."

"Why don't you lend Carson the hat?" Green Riley suggested. "It'll be hard to ignore your best friend when there's

•212•

five of him. Plus, more best friends to go around."

"Thanks, but no thanks," Carson said. "One of me is even too much for me sometimes."

"And there's apparently one hundred Hunters running around out there somewhere," Riley said. "Cloning might not be all it's cracked up to be."

"An understatement," Carson said.

"I guess what I'm trying to say is that it's time to focus on my best friend and my best friend only," Riley said, nudging Carson with her elbow. "Locker 37 didn't give me the power of cloning so I could do a prank. It took me a while, but I figured out that cloning was Locker 37's roundabout, unpredictable way of showing me that the world isn't all about me. So I'm going to have to tell myself—"

"Goodbye," the clones all said at the same time, because they were all on the same wavelength. And all good songs must eventually come to an end.

That's when Riley winked at them and took off her ridiculous and wonderful rainbow hat.

But it didn't freeze the clones this time. It made them disappear.

In fact, it made all the clones (the goldfish and the drones and the Hunters) disappear. It also made all the headbands and hats disappear, including Riley's ridiculous and wonderful rainbow hat.

So Riley's hands were empty.

"You remember when I said you were

predictable?" Carson asked.

"Of course," Riley replied. "I didn't like it. It felt like an insult."

"But it can be a compliment, too," Carson said. "Because I always know that in the end . . . you'll be there for me. That's the best kind of predictable."

Then Carson reached out and grabbed one of Riley's empty hands.

Chapter Thirty-Six
UNIQUE

The Junior Janitor Club, which now included Keisha, Riley, and its newest member, Carson, were in the gym, working hard at stuffing Ping-Pong balls into trash bags.

Don't worry. This is what Carson wanted to do, because it meant spending more time with his best friend. Besides, he was enjoying seeing Riley clean up the prank she had missed.

Reggie Blue stood in the doorway, watching them with his arms crossed. He had offered to help, but they told him he deserved a break and that they'd handle the mess.

Vice Principal Meehan stood next to the janitor, watching as well. He said, "That Junior Janitor Club is a strange club, don't you think?"

"You got that right," Reggie Blue said.

"But it's certainly made a name for itself today, hasn't it?" Vice Principal Meehan said.

Reggie smiled and said, "They're ubiquitous."

Hunter, who had sneaked up behind them, tapped Vice Principal Meehan on the shoulder and said, "What about me? That was my prank. I made the biggest name for myself! I'm the most ub—"

"I've known your name for a while now, son," Vice Principal Meehan said as he pointed to his office. "And you know the drill."

Hunter smiled as he turned around to walk to Vice Principal Meehan's office. Sure, he was about to face some major punishment, but students at Hopewell Elementary would be talking about the prank forever. And they'd be giving Hunter all the credit.

Plus, his mom got an onion tart for her birthday. Things couldn't get any better, as far as he was concerned.

"Things can't get any worse," Keisha

said as she stuffed more Ping-Pong balls into a trash bag.

"What's the matter?" Carson asked.

"I was just in Mrs. Shen's room," Keisha said. "And all of Finn and Gill's babies are gone."

"I doubt that," Bryce said as he entered the gym, carrying the rainbow parachute.

"The parachute!" Carson cried out in happiness.

"I found it in the Dungeon," Bryce said. "The rainbow specter has gone back to whatever dimension it came from. So I bet the same thing is true of those goldfish babies."

"Another dimension?" Keisha asked.

That's when Riley flashed Keisha the Locker 37 hand signal. Two hands, with all her fingers spread wide.

"Oh . . . ," she said. "I see."

"It'll be okay," Riley said. "You still have Finn and Gill. And more of something doesn't always equal better. Besides, you wanna know why I like you all so much?"

"Because we help you do pranks?" Carson asked.

"Because we keep you out of trouble?" Keisha asked.

"Because we don't eat any of your fish sticks?" Bryce asked.

Riley laughed and said, "No. The reason I like you so much is because you're all predictable. But you're also all unique."

Then she put her arms around them, pulled them together in a huddle, and said, "Just like me."

Chapter Thirty-Seven

COMING
NEXT . . .

The wildest, funniest, and bithawest Locker 37 adventure yet!
Don't worry. There will be fish sticks.